Published by
Princeton Architectural Press
202 Warren Street
Hudson, New York 12534
www.papress.com

First published in French under the title: *Merci, Miyuki!*
© 2018, De La Martinière Jeunesse,
a division of La Martinière Groupe, Paris

English edition © 2020 Princeton Architectural Press
All rights reserved
Printed and bound in China
23 22 21 20 4 3 2 1 First edition

ISBN: 978-1-61689-901-1

This book was illustrated using watercolors and colored pencils.

Editors: Amy Novesky and Parker Menzimer

Library of Congress Cataloging-in-Publication Data
available upon request.

TEXT BY
Roxane Marie Galliez

ILLUSTRATIONS BY
Seng Soun Ratanavanh

Thank You, Miyuki

PRINCETON ARCHITECTURAL PRESS

NEW YORK

Lilac dew and mist on the grass, Grandpa wakes early to greet the wind.

Close on his heels, Miyuki tries to mimic him. Arm in the air, right foot lifted. She falls to the ground.
"Grandpa, tai chi is too hard!"

Content and smiling, Grandpa dances slowly, his arms drawing curves in the sky.

Miyuki bounces up and down, restless.
"Grandpa, let's do something else!"

"Patience, Miyuki. Can't you see I'm taking care of myself?" Grandpa asks.
"I can take care of you too, Grandpa. I'll make you some tea!"

Miyuki flutters away quick as a butterfly
to make some tea.

She moves so fast she startles the sleeping
birds on her painted porcelain tea set.

But Grandpa doesn't hear her clattering.

She fills the teapot with cold, clear water
and sets it down next to the chipped teacups
on the garden table.

"Grandpa, it's ready! Grandpa?
Are you sleeping?"

Grandpa sits peacefully, his legs crossed, his eyes closed.
He doesn't move when Miyuki waves a fan, cooling his face.

When he finally opens his eyes, Miyuki freezes in place,
still as a statue.
"What is it, Miyuki?"
"Grandpa, I made some tea for you."
"Thank you, Miyuki, but I just want a moment to meditate."
"What's *meditate*? Is it a game? Teach me! I want to meditate, too!"

Grandpa regards Miyuki with delight and gives her a kiss.
"Very well, Miyuki. Let's drink the delicious tea you kindly made."

Grandpa shares the cold water with Miyuki, paying
close attention to all the flavors she describes, savoring
it as if it were a rare tea.

"When do we start to meditate, Grandpa?"

Without a word, Grandpa stands up and begins to walk
calmly down the garden path. Miyuki follows him.

While Grandpa regards the ground beneath his feet,
Miyuki bounds ahead of him.

"When do we start to meditate, Grandpa?"

Grandpa takes Miyuki's hand, and together they
watch the bees hovering, the stones standing still,
the grass slowly growing.

When they reach the river, Grandpa watches the water. Giggling, Miyuki throws in twigs and watches them float away.

"When do we start to meditate, Grandpa?"

Grandpa seats Miyuki next to him and shows her the light playing on the water.

"Miyuki, look at the water. Not the flow. Not the twigs floating by. Only the water in front of your eyes."

Grandpa lies down in the soft grass
and Miyuki nestles against him.
When Miyuki looks at the clouds, she sees
thousands of shapes.

"I see a fox! A hen! No, a lamb! A horse! A bird!" she shouts.
"What do you see, Grandpa?"

Grandpa smiles, satisfied just to be lying in the warm sun, feeling
each blade of grass beneath him, with Miyuki at his side.

"I see a cloud, Miyuki. A cloud watching a grandfather
and his granddaughter."

Miyuki looks at the clouds again and tries to see just
clouds. But her mind wanders.

"Grandpa, does this little cloud have a grandfather, too?"
"Yes, Miyuki, and I'm sure that he's watching over her."

When little raindrops begin to fall,
Grandpa doesn't move. Laughing,
he opens his mouth to taste them,
and Miyuki does, too.

As the day gets dressed for night, Grandpa and Miyuki take a tranquil walk back home.
In front of the garden gate, Grandpa stops to smell a rose before it closes.

Grandpa shows Miyuki the rose, and she closes her eyes and breathes in its sweet perfume.

"But Grandpa, when will we meditate?"

"Miyuki, we have meditated all day long.

When we walked on the path in silence,
admiring the garden, the bees, the stones,
and the grass, we meditated.
When we sat by the river and looked at
the water in front of us, without following
its flow, we meditated.
When we watched the clouds
without changing them into
anything else, simply
appreciating what we saw,
we meditated."

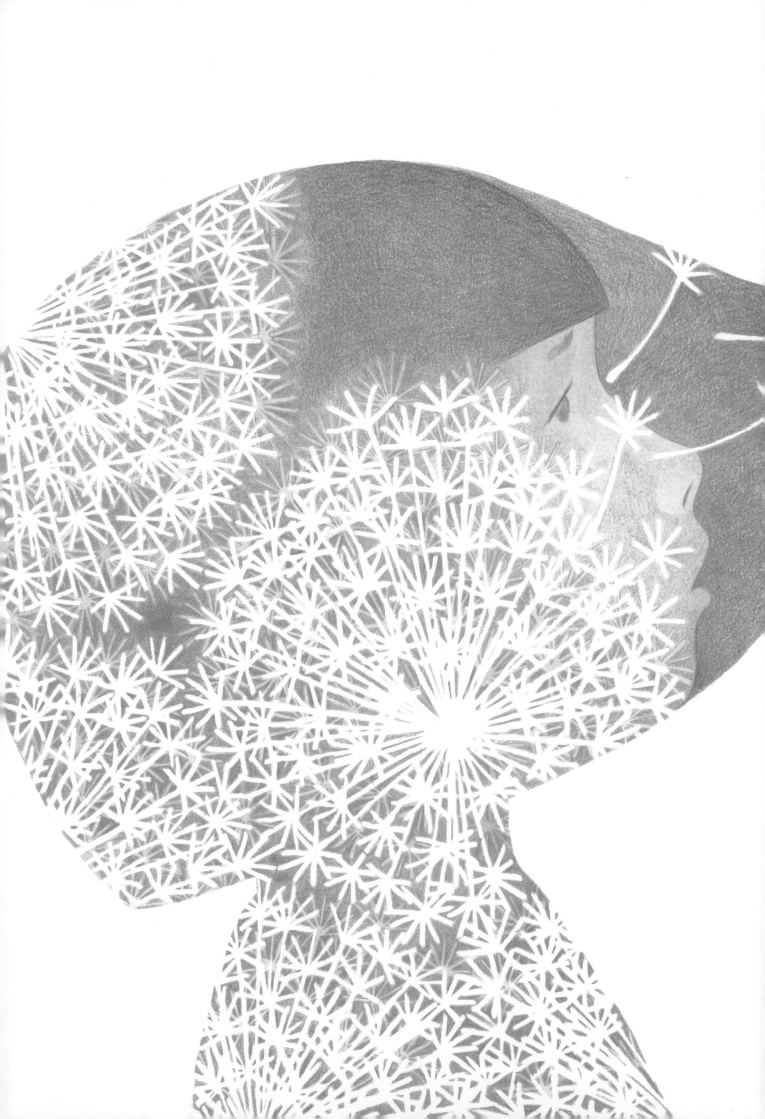

"And when we tasted the tea and the rainwater,
 we meditated?" Miyuki asks.
"Yes, Miyuki."

"And when we smelled the rose we meditated?"
"Yes, Miyuki."

"Grandpa, we have meditated!"
"Yes, Miyuki, we have."

 Miyuki stops and takes Grandpa's hand.
"Grandpa, doesn't it feel good to be here right now?"

"Yes, my dear girl, it feels good to be here right now with you. Thank you, Miyuki."

Grandpa gives her a hug.

And Miyuki breathes in. And Miyuki meditates.